Walt Disney's

Pinocchio

and the Whale

First American Edition

Copyright © 1977 by The Walt Disney Company. All rights reserved under International and Pan-American
Copyright Conventions. Published in the United States by Random House, Inc., New York, and simultane-
ously in Canada by Random House of Canada Limited, Toronto. Originally published in Denmark as
PINOCCHIO OG HVALEN by Gutenberghus Bladene, Copenhagen. Copyright © 1977 by Walt Disney
Productions. ISBN: 0-394-83712-6 ISBN: 0-394-93712-0 (lib. bdg.)   Manufactured in the United States of
America.

Pinocchio, the little wooden puppet, had come home at last.

He and his friend, Jiminy Cricket, had been away for many days.

On the door was a piece of paper.

The paper was a letter from the Blue Fairy.

Dear Pinocchio,

I have very bad news.

Geppetto, your father,

went fishing.

He fell into the sea and was

swallowed by Monstro the Whale.

The Blue Fairy

"My poor father!" cried Pinocchio.
"We must go down to the sea and save him!"

Jiminy Cricket pointed with his umbrella.

"The sea is that way," he said. "But it is miles and miles from here."

"I don't care how far it is," said Pinocchio.

"I have to find Geppetto."

Pinocchio and Jiminy
walked and walked.
They passed through towns.
They passed by shepherds.
And still they went
on and on.

At last they reached the sea.

They stared at it from a high cliff.

"Look at all that water!" said Pinocchio.

"How will we ever find Monstro the Whale?"

"We may as well jump in," said Jiminy Cricket.

They jumped off the cliff into the water far below.

Down they drifted
through a green,
watery world.

The fish were
very surprised
to see
Jiminy
and
Pinocchio.

Soon the wooden boy and the cricket
landed on the bottom of the sea.

"What fun!" cried Jiminy, as they
floated around.

"If we are going
to find Geppetto,"
said Pinocchio,
"we had better start
looking for him."

"Have you seen Monstro the Whale?"
he asked an octopus.

At the sound of Monstro's name, the octopus
swam away in fright.

So did eight little fish.

"Everyone is afraid of Monstro," said Jiminy.
"He must be terrible!"

"Terrible or not, we must keep looking for him,"
said Pinocchio. "We have to save Geppetto."

They kept on walking until they came
to something big and dark.

What could it be? A cave?

It was Monstro—sound asleep!

"We will have to wake him up," said Pinocchio,
"if we want to find Geppetto."

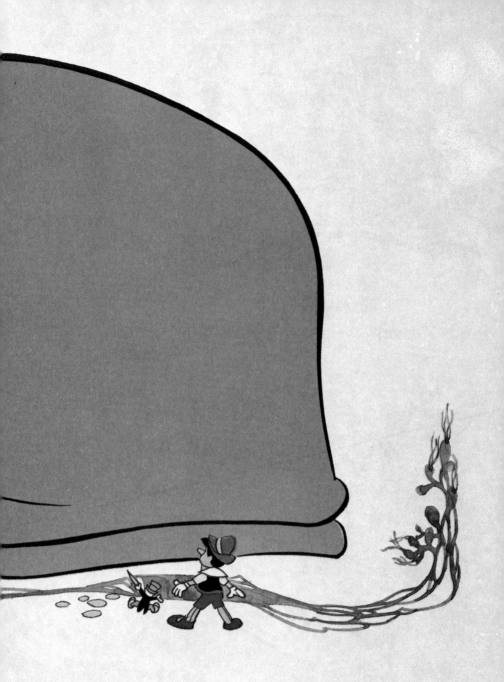

"How do you wake up a whale?" asked Jiminy.
"I think we had better let him sleep."

Just then Monstro opened one sleepy eye.
He was awake—and hungry!

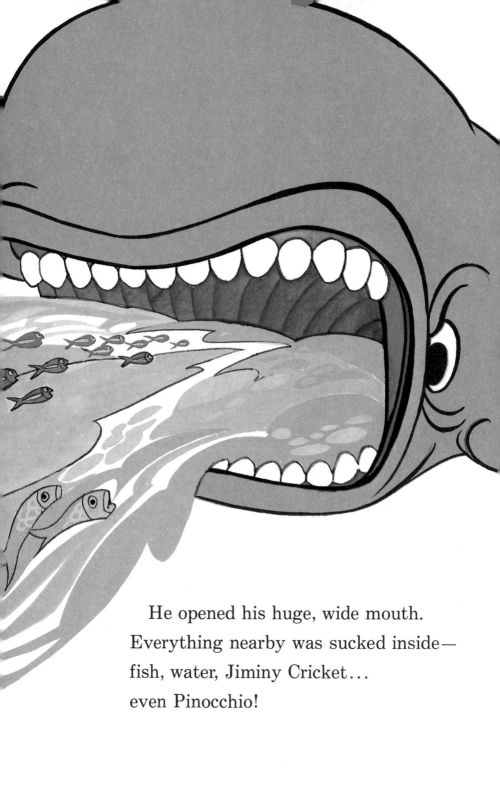

He opened his huge, wide mouth.
Everything nearby was sucked inside—
fish, water, Jiminy Cricket...
even Pinocchio!

The great wave carried them
right into Monstro's belly.

"We did it, Jiminy!" said
Pinocchio. "Now we can
find Geppetto!"

Sure enough, deep inside the whale
was a battered little boat.

On it sat Geppetto, fishing.

Geppetto's cat, Figaro, mewed softly.

"I know you are hungry," Geppetto said.
"If Monstro does not swallow some fish soon,
we will all starve."

Geppetto's pretty goldfish, Cleo,
stared out of her bowl.

She was hungry too.

All at once, great waves rocked
the little boat from side to side.
And Geppetto caught a big fish
on his line.

Then he caught another fish.

It was so big that Geppetto could
hardly pull it in.

No wonder! This time he had caught
Pinocchio and Jiminy Cricket!

"Pinocchio, my son!" cried the happy old man. "Is it really you?"

He hugged the little boy that he had carved out of wood so long ago.

"Father!" said Pinocchio.
"I have come to save you."

"There is no way to get out of here," said Geppetto, sadly.

"I know a way," said Pinocchio.

"First, we must build a raft," he said.

So they went to work with hammers and nails.

"Now we must make the whale open
his mouth," said Pinocchio.

So they
set fire
to Geppetto's
fishing boat.

Hot, black smoke began to fill Monstro's belly.
It tickled his throat and came pouring out
of his mouth.

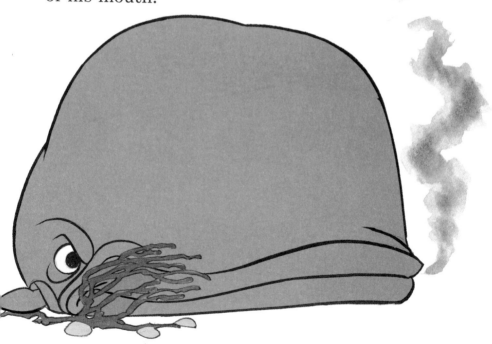

The whale snorted. Then he coughed.
Finally he sneezed—
AH-AH-AH-AH-CHOOOOO!

The raft came shooting out of his mouth.
Pinocchio and Geppetto grabbed the mast
and held on tightly.

Monstro was angry—very angry.

He swam through the water
with his jaws wide open.

The little raft tipped up on one end.

"Watch out!" cried Geppetto.
"He will swallow us again!"

Suddenly they all spilled into the sea—
Geppetto, Cleo, Pinocchio, Figaro,
and Jiminy Cricket.

"Swim for your lives!"
shouted Pinocchio.

Poor old Geppetto soon grew tired.
"Leave me behind," he said.
"Save yourselves."

But Pinocchio put his arm
around Geppetto.
He kept the old man
from sinking.
It was very hard work
for the little wooden boy.

Finally they reached land.
Pinocchio was so tired he could hardly
drag Geppetto out of the water.

He almost fell
right on top of Figaro.

When Geppetto saw Pinocchio
lying there, he sobbed:
"My poor son! You did this
to save my life!"

He picked up
the little wooden boy
and carried him home.

Geppetto put Pinocchio to bed under a warm quilt.
When he saw the little wooden boy lying there
so still, he had to wipe the tears from his eyes.
Figaro, Jiminy, and even Cleo were all very sad.

Suddenly the Blue Fairy
floated into the room.
She touched Pinocchio
with her wand.
"Because you were so brave and thought
of Geppetto instead of yourself" she said,
"I am changing you into a real little boy."

"Look, Father!" Pinocchio cried.
"I am not wooden any more. I am real!"

Geppetto's heart was filled with joy.

He and Jiminy began to play a merry tune, while Pinocchio and Figaro danced a jig.

The Blue Fairy smiled.

She knew that Geppetto had always wanted a real little boy.

At last his wish had come true!